South East England

Edited By Donna Samworth

First published in Great Britain in 2017 by:

Coltsfoot Drive
Peterborough
PE2 9BF
Telephone: 01733 890066
Website: www.youngwriters.co.uk

Foreword

Welcome Readers!

Animals play a crucial role in our world and are loved by us all, it is therefore fitting that for Young Writers' latest competition we asked Key Stage 1 pupils nationwide to put pen to paper and write a poem dedicated to our furry, scaled, slimy or feathered friends.

I'm proud to present Poetry Safari – South East England, a volume that's bursting with incredible verse, from animal acrostics to pet senses this collection has it all. As you begin your tour with us you will also find out some amazing facts on the way, plus you might even find the odd dragon or dinosaur lurking around!

Editing these fantastic poems really was a pleasure and I'd like to congratulate all those that feature within. I hope this gives you all confidence as you begin to get to grips with writing and I look forward to seeing more of your work in the future.

Finally, no more monkeying around, I'll leave you to let your imaginations run wild!

Contents

Chartfield School, Westgate-On-Sea

Jack Shipley (6)	1
Samuel Bird (6)	2
Ellie Hallett (6)	3
Anna Jemima Lindsay-Wood (6)	4
Hadassah Ebimoboere Agama (7)	5
Freddie Pettit (6)	6
George Horsley (6)	7
Alfie Snell (6)	8
Matthew Malone (6)	9

Home Farm Primary School, Colchester

Taylor Gunther (6)	10
Tom Khan (6)	11
Libby Mears	12
Alexi Hayden (6)	13
Nina Hayward (6)	14
Edward Simpson (6)	15
Hannah Knight (6)	16
Charlie Harrison (6)	17
Laila Green (6)	18
Isabel Morton (6)	19
Abigail Garcia (6)	20
Freddy Richer (6)	21
Thomas Gourlay (6)	22
Cameron Gilson (6)	23
Jake Jackson (6)	24
Caeli Nesbitt (6)	25
Holly Hayton (6)	26
Kitty Grindall (6)	27
Jessica Masseti (5)	28

Ellen Crayston (5)	29
Lucie Winnard (5)	30
Alexandra Gray (5)	31
Sienna Lucas (5)	32
Megan Rae Sperring (5)	33
Oscar Hale (5)	34
Sophie Croydon (5)	35
Aimee Margaret Prosser (5)	36
Tom Morton (5)	37
Lola Lappage (5)	38
Lilly Collingridge (5)	39
Maximus Decimus Meridius Peter Farress (5)	40
Lola Cowell (5)	41
Lucas Lachasseigne (5)	42
Charlie Everett (6)	43
Harrison Reuangsak Berry (5)	44
Ethan Cattermole (5)	45
Holly Mobley (6)	46
Hollie Mae Mansfield (5)	47
Jack Stephen Williams (5)	48
Eleanor Turvil (5)	49
Nile Sealey (5)	50
Sidney Woods (5)	51

Northbourne Park Pre-Prep School, Deal

Agatha Hudson (5)	52
Josh Thompson (5)	53
Olivia Victoria Pierce (5)	54
Nancy Holland (5)	55
Lucas Unitt (5)	56
Afraz Malik (5)	57
William Quinn (5)	58
Daniel Thomas Roper Cook (5)	59

Charlie Thompson (5) 60
Grace Harvey (5) 61
Austin William Smith (5) 62
Nathaniel Payne (5) 63

St Nicholas School, Harlow

Joshua Smith (5) 64
Millie Cooke (6) 65
Dilan Patel (6) 66
Chloe Lily Copeman (6) 67
Florence Cunningham-Bryce (6) 68
Honey Florence Dunne (5) 69
Georgina Haigh (6) 70
William Groves (7) 71
Milana Lawrence (6) 72
Grace Hoskin Wise (6) 73
Sylene Hans (5) 74
Henry Cummings (5) 75
Ruby Stradling (6) 76

Tooting Primary School, London

Summer Jessica Rose Reid (5) 77
Freddie Samuel Howarth (6) 78
Zara Gutfreund (6) 80
Melanie Romero (6) 82
William Hoban (6) 83
Stella Desborough (6) 84
Kitty Bouet (6) 85
Nivedha Sudhakar (5) 86
Pragyan (Adi) Chourasia (6) 87
Magdalena Mogavero Garcia 88
Alexa Hall (6) 89
Scarlett Butler (6) 90
Jastin Vecchio (6) 91
Daisy Rolls (6) 92
Charlie Rowe (6) 93
Sharanya Ray (7) 94
Philip Cicovacki (6) 95
Jennah Rumjaun (6) 96
Freya Lee-Snell (6) 97
Beatrix Mary Louise 98
Reddaway (6)

Leon Hyseni (6) 99
Kayla Eden Williams-Edwards (7) 100
Molly Raby (5) 101
Alethea Nutt (5) 102
Maya Jackson Williams (6) 103

Vita Et Pax School, London

Shyla Pathmanathan (6) 104
Abbas Hassan Datoo (7) 106
Amy Edjourian (6) 107
Mia Bowers (7) 108
Nuala Gregg (7) 109
Christopher Polzone (6) 110
Oyinade Oduyemi (5) 111
Sophia Panayi (6) 112
Jonathan Wong (6) 113
Amelie Nosworthy (5) 114
Oluchi Ojike (5) 115
Erin Reilly (6) 116
Aviana Bella Petrou (5) 117

Woodside Academy, Grays

Willow Pixie Jane Hodges (6) 118
Olivia Fitchett (7) 119
Lois Mason Ward (6) 120
Zac Goodman (6) 121
Tehillah Oloyede (6) 122
Brandon Derek Byrne (6) 123
Rudra Ankit Pandya (6) 124
Aimee Byrne (6) 125
Eren Insua-Winfield (6) 126
Alisa Pozdyseva (6) 127
Peyton Mason (6) 128
Grace North (6) 129
Ollie Gray (6) 130
Ruby Grace Watts (6) 131
Rajan Sangha (6) 132
Jack Millane (6) 133
Kye Marley Butler (6) 134
Amy Smethurst (6) 135
Alfie Tilney (6) 136
Taylor-George Anderson (7) 137

Lola Penn (6)   138
Lealand Price (6)   139
Cayden Maccabe (6)   140
Dulcie Pryer (6)   141

The Poems

Polar Bear

P olar bears live in the Antarctic
O ld polar bears live in the Antarctic too
L oud when they roar
A lways searching for prey
R uns very fast

B lack skin but with white fur
E normous polar bears chase the seals
A polar bear runs for miles
R eally big.

Jack Shipley (6)
Chartfield School, Westgate-On-Sea

Polar Bear

P rowl
O ld and tired from hunting
L arge
A polar bear likes meat
R uns very fast

B eautiful
E ats a lot of food
A mazing
R oars loudly.

Samuel Bird (6)
Chartfield School, Westgate-On-Sea

Horse

H orses are beautiful and sweet
O n the head is a mane
R eally fast runners
S leeps in a stable
E ats lots of hay.

Ellie Hallett (6)
Chartfield School, Westgate-On-Sea

The Rabbit

I have a rabbit, he is very small
And he curls up into a ball.
When I am snoring in bed he sits on my
head,
When I wake up I am sitting on his head!

Anna Jemima Lindsay-Wood (6)
Chartfield School, Westgate-On-Sea

Zebra

Z ebras are fast
E xciting when they are in the jungle
B lack stripes
R uns around in Africa
A mazing animals.

Hadassah Ebimoboere Agama (7)

Chartfield School, Westgate-On-Sea

The Tiger

T errifying and hairy
I nteresting and scary
G iant and great
E xcellent and fast
R ough and sleepy.

Freddie Pettit (6)
Chartfield School, Westgate-On-Sea

Cats

C urls up in the sun
A cat climbs trees
T errible hunter at chasing mice
S neaking about the house.

George Horsley (6)
Chartfield School, Westgate-On-Sea

The Panda

P andas are fluffy
A panda climbs trees
N ibble bamboo
D elightful
A panda is cool.

Alfie Snell (6)
Chartfield School, Westgate-On-Sea

The Worm

W riggly worm is in the soil
O ld, kind, good worm
R esting in the soil
M oves really slowly.

Matthew Malone (6)

Chartfield School, Westgate-On-Sea

Discovering Dinosaurs

D eadly T-rex, they were killed a long time ago

I nteresting bones because they are cool

N oisy dinosaurs are very noisy

O ld T-rex was interesting

S tegosaurus has spikes on its back

A wesome T-rex because it is fighting

U nderwater dinosaur

R oaring rumpus.

Taylor Gunther (6)

Home Farm Primary School, Colchester

Discovering Dinosaurs

D ied 1,000 years ago
I mpossible fishing
N o fighting dinosaurs
O i, you can't eat other dinosaurs
S low down dinosaur
A mazing T-rex
U nusual triceratops
R umpers, the silly pterodactyl.

Tom Khan (6)

Home Farm Primary School, Colchester

Discovering Dinosaurs

D inosaurs love hunting
I mpressive dinosaurs are cool
N ice dinosaurs are cool too
O ther dinosaurs live differently
S leeping dinosaurs
A m I a dinosaur?
U p in the sky
R ude dinosaur.

Libby Mears
Home Farm Primary School, Colchester

Discovering Dinosaurs

D iplodocus was very long
I found dinosaur bones
N o dinosaurs nod a lot
O mnivores eat meat and plants
S low diplodocus
A diplodocus ate plants
U gly diplodocus
R upert the diplodocus.

Alexi Hayden (6)
Home Farm Primary School, Colchester

Discovering Dinosaurs

D ied a million years ago

I nteresting tyrannosaurus rex

N oisy stegosaurus

O ld brontosaurus

S wimming plesiosaurus

A terrific triceratops

U nusual names

R oaring tyrannosaurus rex.

Nina Hayward (6)

Home Farm Primary School, Colchester

Discovering Dinosaurs

D ied millions of years ago
I t lived in forests
N oisy diplodocus
O ld diplodocus
S napped the diplodocus
A mazing diplodocus
U nder the ground hidden bones
R ed-hot lava.

Edward Simpson (6)

Home Farm Primary School, Colchester

Discovering Dinosaurs

D ead T-rex years ago

I cy T-rex years ago

N oisy dinosaur

O ld T-rex and dinosaur

S tegosaurus had spikes on his back

A mazing T-rex and bones

U gly T-rex

R oaring T-rex.

Hannah Knight (6)

Home Farm Primary School, Colchester

Discovering Dinosaurs

D ifficult diet
I nteresting, scuttering creatures
N asher and speedy
O h raptors are fast
S kilful creatures
A rchaeologists find bones
U nusual names
R umpus dumpus.

Charlie Harrison (6)
Home Farm Primary School, Colchester

Discovering Dinosaurs

D ied millions of years ago
I t likes to eat plants
N ice dinosaurs
O ut for dinosaurs
S tegosaurus is cool
A wesome dinosaurs
U p in the sky
R unning dinosaurs.

Laila Green (6)
Home Farm Primary School, Colchester

Discovering Dinosaurs

D irty pterodactyl
I mpossible fishing
N oisy pterodactyl
O ld dinosaurs
S oft wings
A mazing pterodactyls
U nusual pterodactyls
R ambling T-rex.

Isabel Morton (6)
Home Farm Primary School, Colchester

Discovering Dinosaurs

D ied a long time ago
I nteresting neck
N o more diplodocus
O ut to get leaves
S uper diplodocus
A mazing bones
U nusual walking
R oaring loudly.

Abigail Garcia (6)
Home Farm Primary School, Colchester

Discovering Dinosaurs

D angerous velociraptor
I can see it
N ot alive anymore
O nly eats meat
S tegosaurus is scary
A lways hungry
U gly faces
R unning in the forest.

Freddy Richer (6)
Home Farm Primary School, Colchester

Discovering Dinosaurs

D ied a million years ago

I nteresting bones

N oisy T-rex

O ld T-rex

S leepy dinosaur

A wesome bones

U nusual dinosaurs

R acing dinosaurs.

Thomas Gourlay (6)

Home Farm Primary School, Colchester

Discovering Dinosaurs

D ied millions of years ago
I nteresting bones
N ot alive anymore
O nly eat meat
S cary and strong
A lways hungry
U gly faces
R un fast.

Cameron Gilson (6)
Home Farm Primary School, Colchester

Discovering Dinosaurs

D inosaurs are cool
I nteresting names
N ot alive anymore
O nly fossils remain
S trong and scary
A ngry and wild
U gly claws
R uns fast.

Jake Jackson (6)

Home Farm Primary School, Colchester

T-Rex

D ied years ago
I mpressive bones
N oisy roars
O ld T-rexes
S ilky T-rexes
A T-rex ate meat
U nkind dinosaurs
R ude dinosaurs.

Caeli Nesbitt (6)

Home Farm Primary School, Colchester

Discovering Dinosaurs

D irty pterodactyl
I ncredible bones
N oisy pterodactyl
O ld pterodactyl
S oft wings
A wkward
U nusual
R umbling bumbling.

Holly Hayton (6)
Home Farm Primary School, Colchester

Discovering Dinosaurs

D inosaurs died
I nteresting velociraptor
N one slow
O ut to hunt
S cary
A mazing speed
U nusual colour
R unning fast.

Kitty Grindall (6)

Home Farm Primary School, Colchester

Cats

C ute kittens purr at you
A ll cats are cunning
T iny kittens are smooth
S cratchy kittens are snarly.

Jessica Masseti (5)
Home Farm Primary School, Colchester

Cats

C rafty cats do acrobats
A hungry cat scratches
T iny kittens lay on your tummy
S ome cats are shabby.

Ellen Crayston (5)

Home Farm Primary School, Colchester

Cats

C ute cats sat on my lap
A ngry cats scratch me
T ouchy cats rub up on me
S habby cats in the mud.

Lucie Winnard (5)

Home Farm Primary School, Colchester

Cats

C ute cats curl up with you
A ngry cats scratch and hiss
T ubby, tall cats
S leepy cats snore.

Alexandra Gray (5)
Home Farm Primary School, Colchester

Cats

C uddly cats jump and purr
A ngry cats scratch me
T iny kittens like me
S ome cats are crafty.

Sienna Lucas (5)
Home Farm Primary School, Colchester

Cats

C rafty cats do acrobatics
A ngry claws scratch
T ubby cats are fat
S illy cats like to jump.

Megan Rae Sperring (5)

Home Farm Primary School, Colchester

Cats

C uddly kitten purrs at me
A ngry and scratchy
T iny and curly tails
S mart cats catch mice.

Oscar Hale (5)

Home Farm Primary School, Colchester

Cats

C rafty cats do acrobatics
A ngry cats scratch
T iny kittens lay
S habby cats roll in mud.

Sophie Croydon (5)

Home Farm Primary School, Colchester

Cats

C ute cats cuddle on my lap
A ll my cats purr
T he cat licks me
S habby cats in my garden.

Aimee Margaret Prosser (5)

Home Farm Primary School, Colchester

Cats

C ute kittens love me
A crobatic cats do tricks
T his cat trusts me
S cratches my head.

Tom Morton (5)

Home Farm Primary School, Colchester

Cats

C ute kittens purr
A ngry cats scratch
T all cats do tricks
S upple cats do acrobatics.

Lola Lappage (5)
Home Farm Primary School, Colchester

Cats

C ute cats are tall
A ngry cats are timid
T iny cats are smart
S mooth cats are tubby.

Lilly Collingridge (5)

Home Farm Primary School, Colchester

Cats

C ute cats are cuddly
A ngry cats hurt me
T ubby cats eat a lot
S mooth cats are soft.

Maximus Decimus Meridius Peter Farress (5)

Home Farm Primary School, Colchester

Cats

C ute kittens
A ngry cats scratch
T ouchy cats scratch
S habby cats roll in the mud.

Lola Cowell (5)

Home Farm Primary School, Colchester

Cats

C ute cats play
A ngry cats scratch
T all cats are smart
S habby cats go in the mud.

Lucas Lachasseigne (5)
Home Farm Primary School, Colchester

Cats

C urly cats are soft
A ngry kittens scratch
T all cats eat mice
S leepy cats snore.

Charlie Everett (6)
Home Farm Primary School, Colchester

Cats

C ute cats purr
A ll cats sleep
T ubby cats are sort of cute
S mooth cats are soft.

Harrison Reuangsak Berry (5)

Home Farm Primary School, Colchester

Cats

C ute cats are fluffy
A ngry cats fight
T all cats are high
S mart cats are bright.

Ethan Cattermole (5)

Home Farm Primary School, Colchester

Cats

C uddly cats purr
A ll cats are cuddly
T iny cats are scratchy
S mooth and slinky.

Holly Mobley (6)
Home Farm Primary School, Colchester

Cats

C ute cats can scratch
A ll cats are cuddly
T iny cats jump a lot
S ome cats purr.

Hollie Mae Mansfield (5)
Home Farm Primary School, Colchester

Cats

C uddly cats do like to play
A ll cats miaow
T imid cats squeal
S ome cats climb.

Jack Stephen Williams (5)
Home Farm Primary School, Colchester

Cats

C ute kittens purr
A ll cats scratch
T iny cats scratch
S cratchy kittens hurt.

Eleanor Turvil (5)

Home Farm Primary School, Colchester

Cats

C ute cats on my lap
A lways funny
T iny paws, tiny feet
S mart, smooth coat.

Nile Sealey (5)
Home Farm Primary School, Colchester

Cats

C ute, cuddly cats
A crobatic cats
T iny and trusting
S mart cats.

Sidney Woods (5)

Home Farm Primary School, Colchester

Giraffe Adventure

G iraffes
I n the jungle
R unning
A nd reaching
F or leaves
F un and
E xciting in the
S un.

Agatha Hudson (5)

Northbourne Park Pre-Prep School, Deal

The Cheetah

C heetahs run fast
H aving fun
E very day
E veryone likes
T hem
A nd they are
H airy.

Josh Thompson (5)
Northbourne Park Pre-Prep School, Deal

The Lost Fox

R ed foxes
E at chickens
D arting through the snow

F ast
O n four legs
'X citing.

Olivia Victoria Pierce (5)
Northbourne Park Pre-Prep School, Deal

The Bunny

B unnies bounce
U p and down
N ice and friendly
N ibbling carrots
Y ummy!

Nancy Holland (5)
Northbourne Park Pre-Prep School, Deal

Scary Shark

S cary
H airy
A ngry
R ace fast through the water
K illing other animals.

Lucas Unitt (5)
Northbourne Park Pre-Prep School, Deal

The Little Jackal

J oking
A ngry
C heeky
K neeling down
A mazing
L ying.

Afraz Malik (5)

Northbourne Park Pre-Prep School, Deal

The Zebra

Z ebras
E at grass
B lack and white
R un
A frica.

William Quinn (5)
Northbourne Park Pre-Prep School, Deal

The Pirate And The Lion

L ying on the grass
I ncredible animals
O bedient
N aughty.

Daniel Thomas Roper Cook (5)

Northbourne Park Pre-Prep School, Deal

Bunny

B unny hops
U p
N aughty
N ibbles
Y ummy.

Charlie Thompson (5)
Northbourne Park Pre-Prep School, Deal

Cat

C ats are big
A nd furry
T hey are cuddly.

Grace Harvey (5)

Northbourne Park Pre-Prep School, Deal

Fruit Bat

B lack
A ngry
T wisting
S ad.

Austin William Smith (5)

Northbourne Park Pre-Prep School, Deal

Bats Fly

B lack
A nd scary
T urning in the sky.

Nathaniel Payne (5)

Northbourne Park Pre-Prep School, Deal

Safari Senses

I can see slithery snakes
I can hear loud lions
I can smell dirty hippos
I can eat bananas like the monkeys do
I can feel long grass where the leopards live

I can see tall giraffes
I can hear tigers roar
I can smell stinky gorillas
I can feel a good fluffy dog
I can taste the cool water where the
elephants drink and play.

Joshua Smith (5)
St Nicholas School, Harlow

Squidgy Octopus Eadon

O range Eadon was in her dark cave
C rossy ate 100 fish to fill her up
T errifying Eadon scared a shark away
O lly Octopus squirts in black ink
P roudly she sneaks into the cave
U nder the cave is a boulder, she gets stuck
S uddenly she cannot move in the cave.

Millie Cooke (6)

St Nicholas School, Harlow

The Cheeky Camel

C reepy, scary camel who comes out
behind a pyramid
A ngry, cute camel
M ouldy skin that is falling off
E normous hump
L oud, talking, bossy camel.

Dilan Patel (6)
St Nicholas School, Harlow

A Safari Senses Poem

I can see a muddy monkey.
I can see a smooth, scaly snake.
I can taste a chewy, slimy snail.
I can hear a loud, soft parrot.
I can smell a loud, long lion.

Chloe Lily Copeman (6)

St Nicholas School, Harlow

Pony

P onies are adorable
O nly I love them millions
N ever smell of roses, always smelly
Y ou would love one too.

Florence Cunningham-Bryce (6)
St Nicholas School, Harlow

A Safari Poem

I can see a gorilla.
I can smell a smelly snake.
I can feel a hard parrot.
I can hear a scary snake.
I can taste a slithery bug.

Honey Florence Dunne (5)

St Nicholas School, Harlow

Pony

P retty, pretty pony
O nly the most dazzling animal
N early as fast as a cheetah
Y ou love to be ridden.

Georgina Haigh (6)
St Nicholas School, Harlow

Shark

S uper fast swimmers
H ungry for food
A ngry animals
R eally dangerous
K iller sharks.

William Groves (7)

St Nicholas School, Harlow

Cat

C ats are crazy and cute

A mazing cats are really cute

T errified cats are scared when people shout loudly.

Milana Lawrence (6)

St Nicholas School, Harlow

Horse

H ungry for hours
O nly one of a kind
R eally huge
S oft and brown
E asy to love.

Grace Hoskin Wise (6)

St Nicholas School, Harlow

Flying Horses

I can see a flying horse.
I can smell my horse.
I can see my horse drinking.
I can see horses flying up in the sky.

Sylene Hans (5)
St Nicholas School, Harlow

Monkey Life

I can see a mother.
I can hear a monkey.
I can feel its soft fur.
I can taste bones.
I can smell bananas.

Henry Cummings (5)
St Nicholas School, Harlow

The Fierce Lion

L oud lion
I rritating, ignoring lion
O range lion
N oisy lion.

Ruby Stradling (6)
St Nicholas School, Harlow

My Friend Fiona

She leaps like a gymnast
When she flies through the air.
I want to give her braids
But she's got no hair.
I want to go to a castle
But Fiona can't walk.
She eats fish but can't use a fork.
We love to play together,
We pretend to drink tea,
Eat cake and swim in the sea.
She swims and she smiles,
She's got a tail.
Have you guessed what she is yet?
No, not a snail!
Flippers and a fin and a happy grin,
She is of course a dolphin!

Summer Jessica Rose Reid (5)
Tooting Primary School, London

The Tiger Protector

Freddie was a tiger protector,
He went to make a film
In a hot Indian forest,
Where fierce tigers roam.

There were two baby tiger cubs
That were playing under the trees,
Their mother was lying next to them,
She was sleeping in the breeze.

Suddenly the cameraman jumped
And shouted, 'Hey, look out!'
There was a poacher creeping along,
He'd kill the tiger no doubt.

As quick as a flash Freddie sprinted
And grabbed his animal dart gun.
He shot it at the poacher
And hit him on the bum.

The tiger rubbed against Freddie
To say thank you and well done.
Then she carried her two cubs away
And strode off in the bright sun.

Freddie Samuel Howarth (6)
Tooting Primary School, London

Safari

Let's go to the safari
And see what we can find.
It might be a gorilla or a hippo.
So let's go to the safari -
What might there be?
Look over there!
It's a long, tall giraffe with its head so high
It almost touches the sky.
Let's walk some more
And find some more animals.
Look over there!
It's a big gorilla.
It munches and chews
And looks so cute until it beats its chest.
So we've seen two animals -
One more to go.
Now what might it be?
Come on let's find out.

Look over there!
It's a big hippo.
It's rolling in thick mud.
Ahh! Look out, the mud is flying right at us!

Zara Gutfreund (6)

Tooting Primary School, London

The Monkeys

Monkeys have a long strong tail,
Either they are male or female.
They are known to be cheeky
And some are very sneaky.
Monkeys live in a rainforest wild and free,
They like to swing from tree to tree.
They like to play and run
To be with other monkeys to have some fun.
Monkeys like to eat fruits and seed
'Cause monkeys know what food they need.
I read a lot of hilarious stories
About furry and funny monkeys.

Melanie Romero (6)

Tooting Primary School, London

Safari In A Ferrari

I went on a safari in a Ferrari,
Let me tell you what I saw.
It was not an elephant, giraffe or a boar,
It was an African hunting dog.
I could tell by his track,
He had brown and black patches all over his back.
So you can keep your lions, tigers and monkeys,
It's an African hunting dog for me.
I would like to keep him for a pet,
But he might eat me for his tea!

William Hoban (6)
Tooting Primary School, London

All About A Giraffe

When giraffes stand they're very high,
It's like their head touches the sky.
Their neck is very, very long,
So that means that their legs are strong.
Giraffes eat shoots and leaves,
They munch on really branchy trees.
Brown spots, long-tongue, black eyes gazing,
I really think they're quite amazing!

Stella Desborough (6)
Tooting Primary School, London

The Gazelle

The gazelle can run very fast
And it can jump very high
Like it's going to kiss a cloud.
Oh, what's that sound?
Oh no, the tiger is on its prowl.
We can hear its growl.
Luckily the gazelle has a very good smell.
Run gazelle, jump gazelle!
Tiger you are unlucky
And you look really mucky!

Kitty Bouet (6)
Tooting Primary School, London

My Friend Giraffe

My giraffe ate my cookies
And drank all my tea
And skated on my skateboard
And climbed in my tree
And while I was sleeping
She played with my toys
And read all my stories
And made all my noise
And woke up my neighbours
But still I forgave her
Because she is my giraffe.

Nivedha Sudhakar (5)
Tooting Primary School, London

Tiger's Life

I see a tiger in the jungle
And he's running fast,
As free as a bird in the sky.
I see a tiger in the jungle
As strong as an elephant.
I see a tiger in the jungle
And his teeth are sharp like a shark.
I see a tiger in the jungle
And he roars loudly, *roar!*

Pragyan (Adi) Chourasia (6)
Tooting Primary School, London

In The Garden

The squirrels climb up the tree
In the night they go to sleep.
The cat hides in the bushes
And in the night he eats fishes.
The fox lives in a hole next to a ball.
The pigeon lives in a nest
And it is the best.
The dog sniffs the floor,
Looking for more.

Magdalena Mogavero Garcia
Tooting Primary School, London

The Giraffe Dance

My giraffe likes to dance and he likes to take a chance.
He likes to loudly sing and eat leafy things.
He's tall and very lean, but he is never ever mean.
He's taller than a tree and he eats leaves.
He has knobbly knees and dances around the trees.

Alexa Hall (6)

Tooting Primary School, London

Penguin

This is a penguin called Binky,
Waddle, waddle, flap, flap.
He likes to waddle and swim in the sea.
Waddle, waddle, flap, flap.
His favourite thing to do is swim with his friends.
Flap, flap, flap, flap.

Scarlett Butler (6)
Tooting Primary School, London

Clever, Clever Tiger

Clever, clever tiger goes to the river to drink.
Clever, clever tiger is so strong.
Clever, clever tiger is so fast he can catch anything.
Clever, clever tiger likes to sleep.
Clever, clever tiger is the real king of the jungle.

Jastin Vecchio (6)

Tooting Primary School, London

All About Flamingos

Flamingos like to hide and play
but when it's night
you might want to snuggle up
with your favourite teddy.
But remember to put a blanket on your
head otherwise you will get pecked by a
flamingo's pointy bit of his beak.

Daisy Rolls (6)
Tooting Primary School, London

The Creeping Tigers

Tigers in the night
Will give you a big fright.
They love to leap,
They love to sleep.
On stripy feet they quietly creep
Through the jungle they hunt their prey,
So better make sure you don't get in their
way.

Charlie Rowe (6)

Tooting Primary School, London

Shiny Peacock

Peacock, how your feathers shine
in the night so divine.
You dance in the rain
with a glow,
by spreading your tail
like a rainbow.
Have you ever heard
that peacock is India's
national bird.

Sharanya Ray (7)
Tooting Primary School, London

Tiger

Tiger, tiger, tiger
Has black stripes.
Tiger, tiger, tiger
Exists in different types.
In the jungle he can hide,
Nobody can see him inside.
Tiger, tiger, tiger,
He's my favourite animal.

Philip Cicovacki (6)
Tooting Primary School, London

A Penguin's Life

A penguin is funny
And cares about its mummy and daddy.
They all live in the cold
Until they are old.
They like to go fishing
But when they aren't
You might find them in the sea swishing.

Jennah Rumjaun (6)
Tooting Primary School, London

Leopard

L azy leopard sleeping in a tree
E yes shut
O range with beautiful black spots
P ouncing and prowling
A nd scary and howling
R un
D eer, run!

Freya Lee-Snell (6)
Tooting Primary School, London

Hippo

A hippo, a hippo, in the swamp,
He plays with his friends
And stamps in the mud.

Oogie, boogie, boogie!
And he eats grass.
Oogie, boogie and splosh!
He jumps in the mud.

Beatrix Mary Louise Reddaway (6)
Tooting Primary School, London

The Lion Who Tried To Roar

The lion tried to roar
But his voice was very sore.
He tried once more
But could not roar.
He didn't know why
And started to cry.
The lion tried
And gave a big fat sigh.

Leon Hyseni (6)
Tooting Primary School, London

Stripy Tiger

My stripy tiger,
It lives in Asia,
It's strong and playful,
But it's in danger.
She has a family,
She's very happy,
Stop killing tigers
And let them be free.

Kayla Eden Williams-Edwards (7)
Tooting Primary School, London

Funky Monkey

My monkey is called Posy.
He is cuddly and cosy.
He lives in the jungle
With his friend Mungle.
Mungle is a red parrot
And they both like to eat carrots.

Molly Raby (5)
Tooting Primary School, London

The Jungle Monster

There was a monster going to the cinema,
He was very tall,
He put on his pyjamas,
He got on a llama
And ate a banana.
He was a very silly monster.

Alethea Nutt (5)
Tooting Primary School, London

The Giraffe Tail

My tail is furry,
It's ever so long.
Watch me swing until it's gone.
I never miss it,
Because it's ever so long.

Maya Jackson Williams (6)
Tooting Primary School, London

Seals

Seals are cute
And they have a newt.

They climb upon a rock
And they wear a filthy sock.

They see pink
And they sometimes sink.

They love ice
And they are very nice.

They are always white
And nearly light.

It jumps down
And stares with a frown.

The sun comes up in the sky
As it eats a fresh chicken pie.

Seals are super right
And they come out in the night.

They play a flute
And they never wear a suit.

Shyla Pathmanathan (6)
Vita Et Pax School, London

A Cheetah

A cheetah, a cheetah,
The fastest runner in the universe.
It's faster than a horse
And as brave as a tiger.
It loves to chase animals at the zoo.
It loves to hunt dogs, it's his favourite meal.
It thinks sleeping is the best.
She's my very good friend.

Abbas Hassan Datoo (7)
Vita Et Pax School, London

My Cat

My cat is fat, it likes food,
Sometimes I think it's rude.
My cat likes to sleep,
So deep it likes to explore
And go out of the door.
My cat likes to dig,
My cat thinks it's big.
My cat is soft,
I take it to the loft.

Amy Edjourian (6)
Vita Et Pax School, London

The Cat

Cats are the best,
They love to rest.

She likes to hunt in the night,
It gives me a fright.

It likes to sleep,
It likes to eat.

My cat is very soft,
She likes to go in the loft.

Mia Bowers (7)
Vita Et Pax School, London

Fun Horse

The fun has started,
It was enchanted.
The horse is cute,
It has four hooves.
It didn't kick me, phew!
It likes the night
But I have a fright.
It eats hay
But I have to say,
I love my horse.

Nuala Gregg (7)
Vita Et Pax School, London

My Cat

My cat is the best.
Its eyes are like dazzling stars in the
moonlight at night.
I love my cat.
My cat loves fresh fish as a dish
And my cat loves to explore.
My cat loves to sleep
And loves to play.

Christopher Polzone (6)
Vita Et Pax School, London

Oh I Love You Giraffe

Oh dear giraffe
How you make me laugh;
With your tall body
That moves so nimbly;
Your long neck reaches high
For leaves in the sky.
Oh I love you giraffe
For how you make me laugh.

Oyinade Oduyemi (5)
Vita Et Pax School, London

All About My Monster The Gruffalo

My monster is fat,
He likes to eat a delicious bat.
His house is made of wood,
He is hairy and scary,
He loves to knock down trees.
He likes to scare people,
He likes to dig in the mud.

Sophia Panayi (6)

Vita Et Pax School, London

The Leopard

Spotty leopard running very fast.
You can hardly see it zooming past.
Hunting in the middle of the night
Giving other animals a fright.

Jonathan Wong (6)
Vita Et Pax School, London

The Dog Is Fierce

The dog is fierce.
The dog is mighty.
He only goes out on the darkest of nights.
You must beware,
He is everywhere.

Amelie Nosworthy (5)
Vita Et Pax School, London

The Crazy Zebra

He's blue
And he's got the flu.
He always needs the loo.
Hopefully not for a number two
Which is a poo.

Oluchi Ojike (5)
Vita Et Pax School, London

My Dog Lexi

My dog is the best.
She loves to have a rest.
She likes to dig.
She is like a big pig.

Erin Reilly (6)
Vita Et Pax School, London

Amanight

He is green.
He can fly.
He has yellow eye.
His name is Amanight.

Aviana Bella Petrou (5)
Vita Et Pax School, London

My Pet Cat

It's as big as a hamster,
It's as fluffy as a rabbit.
It's as smelly as a skunk,
It's as cuddly as a kitten.
It likes to run up a bursting volcano,
Its favourite food is ice cream.
It is my pet cat.

Willow Pixie Jane Hodges (6)
Woodside Academy, Grays

The Cat

It's as funny as a frog,
It's as cheeky as a monkey.
It's as sweet as a teddy bear,
It's as cute as a mouse.
It's as fast as a turtle,
It's as fluffy as a cloud.
It's my funny pet cat.

Olivia Fitchett (7)
Woodside Academy, Grays

The Giraffe

It's as big as a dinosaur,
It's as yellow as the sun.
It's as spotty as a ladybird,
It's as hairy as a bear.
It's as tall as a giant,
It's as slow as a penguin.
It's a giraffe.

Lois Mason Ward (6)
Woodside Academy, Grays

The Sabretooth Tiger

It's as cheeky as a chimpanzee,
It's as furry as a cat.
It's as big as a volcano,
It's as serious as the police.
It's as long as the Shard,
It's a sabretooth tiger.

Zac Goodman (6)
Woodside Academy, Grays

The Hamster

It is as fluffy as a cat,
It's as cute as a mouse.
It is as fast as a cheetah,
It's as kind as a dog.
It is as friendly as a bird,
It's as hungry as a lion.
It's a hamster.

Tehillah Oloyede (6)
Woodside Academy, Grays

The Pet Tiger

He is as big as a mouse,
He is as sweet as an orange.
He is as cheeky as a cat,
He lives in the jungle.
He is as naughty as a baboon,
He is as funny as a dog.
He is a pet tiger.

Brandon Derek Byrne (6)
Woodside Academy, Grays

The Fish

It's as small as a rock,
It swims as fast as a cheetah.
It lives in the bottom of the ocean,
It leaps as high as a tiger.
It is as playful as a pony,
It is a colourful fish.

Rudra Ankit Pandya (6)
Woodside Academy, Grays

The Fluffy Dog

It's as funny as a clown.
It's as white as snow.
It's as fast as a cat.
It's as cute as a baby.
It's as cheeky as a tiger.
It's my fluffy dog.

Aimee Byrne (6)
Woodside Academy, Grays

The Lion

It's as hairy as a rabbit,
It is as scary as a ghost.
It is sweet like a cat,
It is as fast as a cheetah.
It is gigantic like an elephant,
It is a lovely lion.

Eren Insua-Winfield (6)
Woodside Academy, Grays

The Parrot

It's as funny as a monkey,
It's as beautiful as a rainbow.
It's as little as a stick,
It glides like a plane.
It screams like a baby,
It is a parrot.

Alisa Pozdyseva (6)
Woodside Academy, Grays

The Headless Horse

It is as scary as a mummy,
It is as big as a plant.
It is as fast as a cheetah,
It is as fat as an elephant.
It is as smooth as a rhino,
He is a headless horse.

Peyton Mason (6)
Woodside Academy, Grays

The Goose

She is as pretty as a kitten.
She is as fast as a cheetah.
She is as beautiful as a bee.
She lives in the rainforest.
She eats yummy bamboo.
She is a goose.

Grace North (6)
Woodside Academy, Grays

The Bearsnake

It has a long body,
It's as scary as a haunted house.
It's as creepy as a ghost,
It's as fast as a helicopter.
It's a long, scary bearsnake.

Ollie Gray (6)
Woodside Academy, Grays

The Snake

It's as long as a ruler,
It's very brown and red.
It's cool,
It's amazingly funny.
It's got spiky teeth,
It's a stripy snake.

Ruby Grace Watts (6)
Woodside Academy, Grays

My Pet Wolf

He is as fast as a train,
He is as fluffy as a blanket,
He works in a pack,
He hunts for food,
He is the scariest thing in the world,
He is my pet wolf.

Rajan Sangha (6)
Woodside Academy, Grays

My Pet Dinosaur

He has got sharp teeth,
He has got sharp claws,
He lives in the caves.
He is as big as a house,
He is as angry as a shark.
He is my pet dinosaur.

Jack Millane (6)
Woodside Academy, Grays

The Giraffe

It's as tall as the sky,
It's as greedy as a pig.
It's as fat as a baboon,
Its mouth is as small as an ant.
It is a giraffe.

Kye Marley Butler (6)
Woodside Academy, Grays

The Happy Monkey

He is as funny as a clown,
He is as cheeky as a bunny rabbit.
He is as fast as a lion,
He is as cute as a hippo.
He is a happy monkey.

Amy Smethurst (6)
Woodside Academy, Grays

The Giraffe

He is as tall as a house,
He is as big as a tree.
He is as spotty as a cheetah,
He is as fast as a car.
He is a big yellow giraffe.

Alfie Tilney (6)
Woodside Academy, Grays

The Dog

It is as fast as a motorbike,
It is as sleepy as a lion.
It's as fluffy as a rabbit,
It is as cute as a bear.
It is a dog.

Taylor-George Anderson (7)

Woodside Academy, Grays

The Dog

It is as fluffy as a mouse,
It is as scary as a mouse.
It is as wild as a horse,
It is as humongous as the Shard.
It is a dog.

Lola Penn (6)
Woodside Academy, Grays

The Giraffe

It is as tall as a crane,
Its legs are as long as the Great Wall of China.
It is as playful as a bouncy ball,
It is a giraffe.

Lealand Price (6)
Woodside Academy, Grays

The Puppy

It's as dark as the night,
It's as fast as a rhino.
It's as small as a dog bed,
It's a funny, black puppy.

Cayden Maccabe (6)
Woodside Academy, Grays

The Cat

It likes to jump in the mud,
It's as cheeky as a monkey.
It's as sweet as a teddy bear,
It's a cat.

Dulcie Pryer (6)
Woodside Academy, Grays

Young Writers Information

We hope you have enjoyed reading this book – and that you will continue to in the coming years.

If you're a young writer who enjoys reading and creative writing, or the parent of an enthusiastic poet or story writer, do visit our website www.youngwriters.co.uk. Here you will find free competitions, workshops and games, as well as recommended reads, a poetry glossary and our blog.

If you would like to order further copies of this book, or any of our other titles give us a call or visit **www.youngwriters.co.uk**.

**Young Writers, Remus House, Coltsfoot Drive, Peterborough, PER2 9BF
(01733) 890066**

info@youngwriters.co.uk